The Responsibilitree

Written by Claire Saeli May

Illustrated by Anastasia Khmelevska

Growing Up Greatful LLC
www.growingupgreatful.com

For more information, please contact:
Growingupgreatful@gmail.com
Library of Congress Control Number: 2020910665

Hardcover ISBN: 978-1-64921-514-7
Paperback ISBN: 978-1-64921-506-2

Printed in the USA

Dedication

To all of the kind hearted people who spend their days taking care of others, thank you.

"A single act of kindness throws out roots in all directions, and the roots spring up and make new trees."

-Amelia Earhart

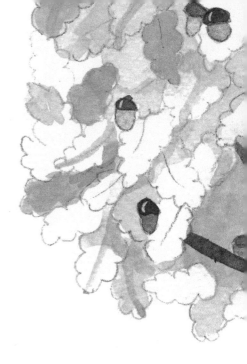

The Mighty Old Oak

is a sight to behold

and has a story,

a lesson,

that now will be told.

He began as an acorn a squirrel picked from a tree
and carefully planted where no one would see.

"Do the right thing--grow tall, be strong,"
Squirrel encouraged and then scurried along.

Acorn appreciated these words, for now he knew

of his responsibility and the things he had to do.

He worked hard to sprout to create a new tree,

reaching and stretching so others could see.

"Be like us,"
the nearby Oaks
would advise,

"forest friends
will be watching
and they're
helpful and wise.

Grow your roots deep
        into the rich, fertile ground,
soak in the water that lies all around.

Stand tall and be proud,
        for you are a special one.
                Your lifetime of growing
has just begun."

The Oak Tree welcomed all
of these encouraging words,
and listened to others,
even the Birds:

"Unfold your leaves,
let them feel the sun's rays.
This warmth will sustain you
through cold, wintry days."

Soon this tiny Oak was tall,

just like his friends,

and though his story had started,

this is **not** where it ends.

In swooped the Wise Owl who was watching for seasons,
proud of this fine tree for so many reasons.

But the Wise Owl knew that it was now his turn
to point out to his friend what he still needed to learn.

"Continue to grow, you are well on your way,

but remember all those that helped you get to today.

You were never alone, others showed that they cared.

Think of the smiles and lessons they shared.

Now, it is your turn to help those in need.

Go out and *pay it forward* with a kind word or deed.

Remember the Squirrel who gave you a start

and the Trees who stood by you and all did their part.

They gave their advice, just like the Birds.

There was so much power in their helpful words."

Hearing this made the Oak stand up straighter,

for he knew the responsibility he had was now so much greater.

He looked all around to see what others might need,

then made his decision—it was time to proceed.

So, he called to his friends to let them all know

he was going to help them all prosper and grow.

Oak offered acorns
to those needing
to eat,

and smiled
as he
watched them
each gather
their treat.

He provided shelter
for all down below
keeping them covered
from wind,
rain,
and snow.

"Come friends,
use my branches
and build your nests.
I am proud to protect you
while you grow and rest."

The friends were grateful for
their kind Oak big brother,
and now were determined to
do something nice for another.

Just like the Mighty Oak,
you can help those in need,
and now it is your turn
to be helpful and do a kind deed!

MIGHTY
OLD
OAK

About the Author

Claire Saeli May is the author of *Santa's Fairy Helpers*.
She treasures her childhood memories of growing up in a
love-filled home with her parents and six older siblings, and
knows that this is where she learned many
valuable life lessons.

Claire lives in Buffalo, NY with her husband Joe, and has
three children: Eric, Brigit, and Alex. She is proud to see they
have each grown to be kind-hearted, responsible adults!

About the Illustrator

Becoming a children's book illustrator has been Anastasia Khmelevska's dream ever since she was a young girl. She has always loved designing characters and painting happy, playful scenes for children. Anastasia lives in Lviv, Ukraine, near her family. Every day she finds inspiration in the little things that surround her.

CPSIA information can be obtained
at www.ICGtesting.com
Printed in the USA
BVHW021110191220
595975BV00002B/32